MESSAGE
BOTTLE

COLESHILL *C of E*
PRIMARY SCHOOL
AND NURSERY

Written by Nikki Sheehan

Illustrated by Felicia Whaley

Collins

Chapter 1

Every morning on their way to school, Cherry and her mum walked along the beach. It was Cherry's favourite place in the world. But every day the sea washed in rubbish and made it messy. So, on Fridays, Cherry and her mum would set out early to tidy it up.

There were so many things that people didn't want anymore. There were also things that had accidentally become rubbish. Cherry had found two faded toothbrushes and some sunglasses with the lenses missing. Once her mum found a pair of false teeth!

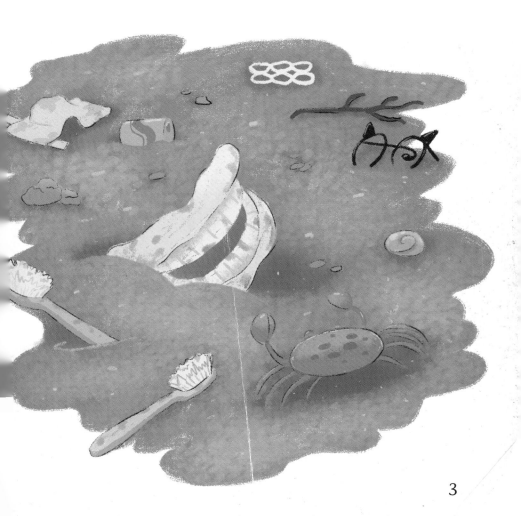

While she was collecting rubbish and lost things, Cherry often found wonderful things too. There were stones with holes through the middle, shells and fossils. Sometimes she found sea glass – pieces of bottles as cloudy as mints.

Cherry would hide her special finds in her school bag, and later she would put them in her treasure chest. She loved her treasures, but she knew that one day she would find something even more special. Maybe gold coins from a pirate ship, a ruby ring, or even a mermaid's mirror.

That Friday morning, it was raining hard. Instead of searching the beach, Cherry and her mum had to walk to school fast so they wouldn't get soaked.

"Hurry up," said Mum, but Cherry was desperate to slow down. The storm in the night had thrown up so many interesting things that it was hard not to investigate everything she saw.

In the distance, Cherry spotted their lovely neighbour, Mr Kovacs, cleaning the beach. He waved at them with his pick-up stick. Cherry let go of Mum's hand so she could wave back. She wished that they could stop and join him.

It was then that Cherry saw it lying on top of the sand, as if it had been waiting for her. It was a bottle, small enough to fit into her hand, the glass misted from being bashed by waves and stones.

"Cherry!" shouted Mum. "No stopping for anything today!"

Cherry stared down at the bottle. She had a funny feeling about it. The kind of feeling she got when she found one of her treasures. She knew that she couldn't leave it. So, without her mum noticing, Cherry picked up the bottle and put it in her coat pocket.

Chapter 2

Cherry was going to tell her mum about the bottle, but it was so blowy on the beach that the wind snatched their words away. Then, when they got to school, Cherry had to run straight into class.

By breaktime, the rain had become a light drizzle. The children all struggled into their waterproofs and ran outside to play. As Cherry buttoned up her coat, she felt the little hard lump in her pocket. It took a moment for her to remember what it was.

Reaching in, Cherry pulled out the bottle. She smiled to herself and held it up to the light, trying to see through the frosted glass.

"Run, Cherry!" shouted her friend Daisy from outside. "Or you won't get picked for the game!" But that day Cherry didn't want to play the game. She wanted to investigate what was inside the bottle and she wanted to do it in private.

"Just a minute," Cherry called to her friend. "I'm doing up my buttons!" she said, although she wasn't really.

I can help you," said Daisy, coming back to the door.

Cherry put the bottle in her pocket. "No," said Cherry. "Start the game without me. I'll be there soon."

Cherry took the bottle out again. The metal top was rusted and stiff. Fortunately, she had very strong arms from doing handstands, so it came off quite easily. She put the top in her pocket so she didn't lose it. Then, peering with one eye inside the bottle, she gasped.

It was exactly what she was hoping for.

Just then, one of the playground supervisors came into the cloakroom.

"Come on, Cherry," she said. "Join the others now."

"OK," said Cherry and, with the bottle held tightly in her hand, she ran straight to the nature area where no one could see her.

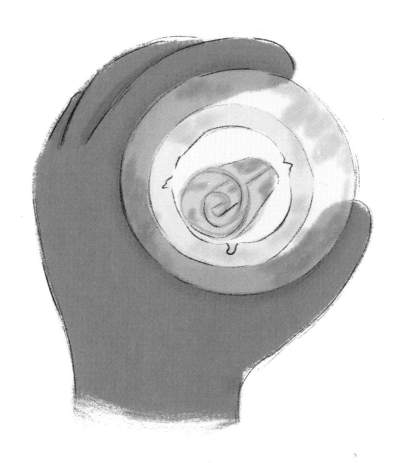

Finally, Cherry was alone and could investigate properly.
The neck of the bottle was too small even for her
smallest finger, so Cherry found a stick and gently
poked until a tiny roll of paper came out.

"I knew it!" Cherry whispered to herself.
"It's a message in a bottle!"

Carefully, Cherry unrolled the paper and began to read.

Dear stranger, I don't know what to do.
I'm eight years old and every day I play alone.
They don't let me join in, and I feel sad.
Can you help me?

S

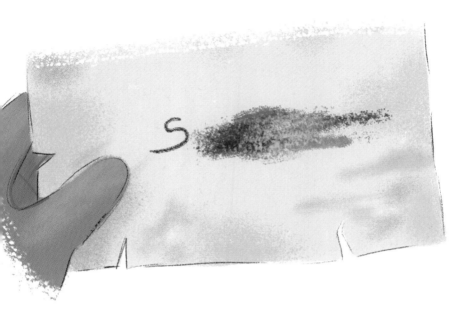

Cherry puzzled over the inky smudge at the end,
but it was impossible to read. Sea water had washed
the person's name away. Everything apart from
the letter "S" had gone.

Cherry thought about whoever had written the note, and the corners of her mouth turned down. She had lots of good friends who always let her play, and it was unfair for anyone to be left out. She decided to find out who had sent the message and become their friend.

"I must think like a detective," she told herself, looking at the playground. But there were so many children out there! How would she find the right person?

The only clues she had were that whoever wrote the note was eight, the same as her, and their name began with an "S".

She looked very carefully, and suddenly Cherry began to notice the children who weren't playing with anyone else. There was Harry who was standing by the wall. But his name didn't start with an "S". And Freya, who was sitting on the friendship bench. But it couldn't be her either.

Then Cherry noticed Cecily from her class. She was sitting on a toadstool reading a book. "It must be her!" Cherry thought, and she ran over and sat down next to her.

"Hello!" said Cherry. "I've come to play with you."

Cecily looked up from her book. "Sorry, Cherry. I can't play right now. I need to finish this chapter, and it's quite long. Maybe tomorrow?"

Then Cherry noticed the label on her school bag.
Cecily's name started with a "C" not an "S"!

So it wasn't her either.

Chapter 3

That afternoon, Cherry listened very carefully when Miss Hurley called out the register. She realised that there were three children in her class whose names began with an "S". Now she was sure that she would find the person who had sent the message.

Stefan

Sam

Sofia

The class began to get ready for their art lesson, putting on aprons and mixing paint. But Cherry didn't join in. She couldn't see Sofia, but she was watching Sam and Stefan. Neither of them looked sad, but Cherry knew that sometimes people hide their feelings.

As the class settled down, Sam was alone working on a drawing of a house. Cherry stood next to him and began to draw too.

"I like the way you draw tiles," she said, because she did.

"Thanks," said Sam, but he didn't even look up.

"Shall I join in?" she asked. "That's going to take you ages."

"No thanks," said Sam.

Sam didn't need her help, so Cherry moved over to Stefan who was making a train out of clay.

"That's really good," said Cherry, because it was. "Can I help? I'm good at making wheels. I make snakes and then I roll them up."

Just then, Raif came over with some wheels he had already made and added them on to the train.

"Sorry," said Stefan. "I'm working with Raif."

The only person left was Sofia. Cherry looked for her everywhere. She wasn't at any of the tables, or by the sink. Cherry even looked under the tables. But she wasn't there either.

"Cherry!" the teacher said loudly. "I've been watching you wandering around all lesson. Please get up off the floor and find something to do by yourself."

"I was looking for Sofia," Cherry explained.

"Sofia is away today," said Miss Hurley. "Now please settle down."

Cherry felt upset at being told off when she had only been trying to help. But she sat down next to Jack and began to try old-fashioned writing with ink and a feather.

Cherry tried to concentrate, but she couldn't stop wondering who had sent the letter. *There must be another clue in the message*, she thought to herself. And then, staring at her old-fashioned handwriting, she suddenly knew the answer! She would look for someone whose writing matched the writing on the note!

Chapter 4

After school, Cherry pretended to leave with everyone else, waving goodbye to her friends and her teacher. Then she sneaked back into the classroom and began to gather up everyone's handwriting books.

She laid them out on the desk. Then, using
the magnifying glass from the nature table,
she compared the letters.

"Cherry! What *are* you doing?"

Cherry spun around. Miss Hurley was standing in the doorway and she did not look happy.

"Oh!" said Cherry. And she tried to think of an answer, but the only answer she could think of was the truth.

"I'm trying to find out who needs a friend," she told her teacher.

Cherry showed Miss Hurley the bottle and the tiny message inside.

"Oh, Cherry," her teacher said. "You are a very kind girl, but I don't think that the person who wrote that message will be in this class."

Miss Hurley took the globe down from the shelf and showed her where their little village is. Then she showed her the big blue sea that led to many other countries. She told her that messages in bottles can travel to the other side of the world and take years and years to reach land. "One famous message took 132 years to arrive," said Miss Hurley.

Cherry thought for a moment. "But the note is written in English so it must have come from a country where they speak English."

"Good thinking, Cherry!" said Miss Hurley, and together they looked at all the countries they could think of where English is spoken. Cherry thought of America, Canada and Jamaica, and Miss Hurley thought of Australia, Zimbabwe and Uganda, though Miss Hurley said that they speak other languages there too.

It was very interesting, but it didn't help Cherry or the lonely child.

She thanked Miss Hurley and went home feeling worried.

Cherry could not eat her dinner. For some reason her tummy felt full, even before she sat down.

"Don't you like spaghetti?" her mum asked,
but Cherry didn't want to tell her the truth about why she was sad and couldn't eat because she didn't want to be in trouble again.

That night there was another storm. It was even worse than the night before, and Cherry didn't sleep well. She could hear the wind whistling and she dreamt about a lonely child in another country shivering in the rain.

Chapter 5

In the morning, golden rays reached inside Cherry's room and woke her up. Finally, it was a sunny day.

Cherry's mum appeared at her doorway. "Come on, sleepyhead," she said. "The beach will be messy after that storm. I've already seen Mr Kovacs on his way with his big bag. I know it's not a Friday, but how about we go and help him?"

Usually Cherry loved cleaning the beach with Mr Kovacs, but even that didn't cheer her up.

After breakfast, they put on their raincoats and boots just in case it rained again, and they walked to the beach.

Mr Kovacs was hard at work when they arrived. He called Cherry over to show her a huge jellyfish that he had found. It was the biggest one that Cherry had ever seen. But Cherry still felt sad.

"Cherry," said Mr Kovacs, "why the long face today?"

Cherry was so full of sadness now that the story poured straight out of her mouth. She told Mr Kovacs about the bottle and the lonely child and getting in trouble at school. Then she got the message out of her pocket and showed it to him.

Mr Kovacs read the note and, to Cherry's surprise, he smiled an enormous smile and then he laughed out loud.

Cherry felt cross. "Someone being sad isn't funny!" she said. But Mr Kovacs put his arm around her shoulders and then he told her a story.

"I came to this country when I was just a little boy. It was a big shock. I'd left all my friends behind. Sometimes I was very lonely. One day, I wrote my feelings in a message. I was going to throw it into the sea but the tide was coming in, so I hid it just by the rocks over there. When I came back, I couldn't find it. That was over 50 years ago! The storm the other day must have finally uncovered it."

Cherry was shocked. "So you're 'S'?"

He smiled. "Yes, I was known as Samson in those days, before I got old and everyone began to call me Mr Kovacs."

"But you're the happiest person I know!" said Cherry.

"The day I wrote it the boys had said I couldn't play football because they thought I cheated. I was very upset," he told her. "I waited and waited for a reply to my message, but none came."

Cherry felt very bad for Mr Kovacs.

"Don't look so worried," said Mr Kovacs. "Soon after that things got better. For one thing, I learnt the football rules." He laughed. "We still have a football team," he said. "And I still cheat sometimes," he added in a whisper.

Cherry smiled. She had solved the mystery and her work was done. Well, almost.

That evening, Cherry wrote a message in her best handwriting and her mum helped her to seal it tight in a tiny bottle.

But Cherry didn't want to make the beach messy, so instead she found somewhere more useful to leave it.

The message said:

Sometimes the days are cold and rainy

and we feel alone and sad. But don't

give up. The sun will always shine

again and everything will get better.

I promise.

From your friends,

Cherry and Samson

X

Cherry's top tips
for keeping the beach clean

1. Even if you don't live near the sea, your rubbish can end up in the sea or on the beach, and harm wildlife. So try to use containers that can be recycled. And say no to plastic straws; they can get stuck up turtles' noses!

2. When you visit the beach, take all your rubbish home with you. Leave only your footprints!

3. If you have gloves like me, or a litter picker like Mr Kovacs, pick up anything that doesn't belong on the beach naturally. And never throw bottles, even ones with messages inside, into the sea!

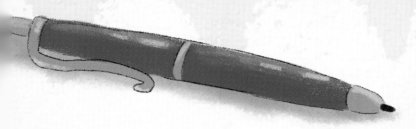

Ideas for reading

Written by Clare Dowdall, PhD
Lecturer and Primary Literacy Consultant

Reading objectives:
- discuss the sequence of events in books and how items of information are related
- make inferences on the basis of what is being said and done
- predict what might happen on the basis of what has been read so far
- explain and discuss their understanding of books, poems and other material, both those that they listen to and those that they read for themselves

Spoken language objectives:
- give well-structured descriptions and explanations
- use spoken language to develop understanding through speculating, hypothesising, imagining and exploring ideas
- participate in discussions, presentations, performances and debates

Curriculum links: Science – living things and their habitats

Word count: 2490

Interest words: message, sea glass, old-fashioned writing, magnifying glass

Resources: paper and pencils; whiteboard and pens; ICT for research, materials for posters (large sheets of paper, colouring pens)

Build a context for reading

- Look at the front cover and read the title *Message in a Bottle*.
- Challenge children to imagine what might happen if they found a bottle with a message in it on a beach, and what they would do.
- Read the blurb to the children and ask them to predict what the message in the bottle might say.

Understand and apply reading strategies

- Read Chapter 1 together, inviting children to take turns reading.
- Invite a volunteer to describe the setting and events at the beginning of the story.